AF248696

JUDY FISKIN

SOME MORE ART

SOME ART

MORE ART

SOME ART

1. Wedgwood plaque with a scene from *The Iliad*, 1990

2. Detail of a painting by Tony Greene, 1989

3. Embossed metal paintings, county fair, 1989

4. Anonymous painting, county fair, 1989

5. Anonymous painting, arts festival, 1990

6. Needlepoint, county fair, 1990

7. *Girl with Tulip*, paint and dyes on wood, Sandy Hubshman, 1990

8. Anonymous woodcarving, 1990

9. Etched glass lamps, 1989

MORE ART

1. Wax effigy of Louis XIV, Musée Grévin, Paris, 1991

2. Reproduction from Hepplewhite's *Cabinet-Maker and Upholsterer's Guide,* 1991

3. Detail of a nineteenth-century sand painting of George Washington's tomb, 1991

4. Anonymous painting in a knot frame, 1992

5. Nineteenth century mosaic, view of Rome, 1992

CREDITS

This book is published on the occasion of the exhibition, "Judy Fiskin: Some Photographs, 1973-1992," at The Museum of Contemporary Art, Los Angeles, October 18 - December 6, 1992. The exhibition, curated by Ann Goldstein, is part of the Museum's "Focus" series.

Presentation of "Judy Fiskin" at MOCA is made possible in part by a generous gift from The Chase Manhattan Private Bank.

Judy Fiskin would like to give special thanks to Patricia Faure of AsherFaure, Los Angeles, to Deborah Irmas, and to Jon Wiener.

This publication has been organized by Russell Ferguson and Sherri Schottlaender, designed by John Campbell, and printed by Typecraft, Inc., Pasadena.

© The Museum of Contemporary Art, Los Angeles, 250 South Grand Avenue, Los Angeles, California 90012.

ISBN 0-914357-28-X